BENEDICT BROWN

A CORPSE IN A
CARAVAN

IZZY PALMER NOVELLA ONE

Copyright

To my wife Marion,
my daughter Amelie
and my accomplice Lucy.

Welcome Note

Hello there! Thanks so much for downloading this brief introduction to the world of Izzy Palmer. I've tried to create a spoiler-free, standalone mystery to whet your appetite but it does take place after the events of the first two Izzy Palmer novels **"A Corpse Called Bob"** and **"A Corpse in the Country"**. If you'd like to find out all that Izzy has been through up to this point, you should check out those books at **Amazon**.

The Campsite

I needed to get away from everything and everyone. I had to escape from all the lies and drama, from dead bosses and potential boyfriends and any question of right and wrong.

Some people would have jetted off to the Bahamas or set sail on a private yacht. I had £100,000 freshly deposited in my bank account, but I wasn't about to waste it. Nope, I didn't have that luxury, but I did have an ex-neighbour with a caravan on the south coast of England.

Hastings is a great place to visit when the sun is shining. It has a Victorian pier and a crumbling castle overlooking the sea. I have happy memories of running along its picturesque high street and raiding the old-fashioned sweetshops in search of sherbet lemons as a child. It turns out that it's not quite so charming in darkest September, with the rain coming down and flood levels rising.

I arrived on a Wednesday, with the sky so grey it looked as if a fleet of alien spaceships had invaded. Walking over to Danny's static caravan was like wading through a swamp. One corner of the box on stilts had sunk towards the turf and a stream of water was cascading from the roof.

I dragged my over-packed suitcase along the sodden path and teetered up the steps. It was good to get out of the rain but my home for the week was only fractionally warmer than outside had been. I put my bags on the floor and attempted to shake myself dry, sheepdog style.

Taking in the space, I could see two bunk beds, a bathroom the size of a phone box, a kitchen the size of a wardrobe and a dinner table with a sofa trapped beneath it. Everything in there was an off-beige colour that it was hard to imagine had ever been fashionable. Not that I cared about any of that. All I required from my holiday was solitude. I wanted to hide away from the world and feel hard done by.

I should have known it was wishful thinking. Five minutes after I arrived, there was a knock at the door.

"Gosh! You're a tall girl." This was all I needed to hear to identify the middle-aged man with curly brown hair and thick-lensed glasses as

Malcolm, the campsite manager. Danny had warned me that Malcolm generally said whatever popped into his head. "I suppose it's handy for cleaning spiders' webs."

"I guess so." I surprised myself by replying with such civility.

"You must be Izzy." He pushed his glasses up his nose, apparently oblivious to the channels of water racing down them. "Your friend told me you were coming. Nice to have some young blood around and all that. Don't even get families here at this time of year."

He motioned to the near-deserted field behind him. "Over in the far corner are Debbie and Roger Harrison. Anwar has the plot next to theirs, though I'll be honest they don't get along. The fancy trailer opposite belongs to Mrs Florence Gaskell and your neighbour here is Birdy."

I peered through the darkness at a shabby grey caravan with a faint glow coming from one window. I'd barely seen it when I arrived and failed to notice the large woman in a waterproof poncho braving the elements beneath a green and white awning.

"Evening." Speaking softly, the small mountain began to stir and make her way over to us. "I didn't want to startle you before so I didn't say hello."

"I'm Izzy Palmer."

"Maureen Collins," she replied. "But everyone calls me Birdy."

Up close, I could see that her youthful voice belied her age. She was in her seventies and wore her long, grey hair in a carefully woven plait like a scarf around her neck. It was the only typically feminine thing about her. For the most part, she looked like an army general or perhaps a tank.

"Terrible weather we're having," Malcolm informed us, because we're British and it's the law.

"Terrible." Birdy looked up at me expectantly.

They want you to invite them in, my brain said.

Yes, thank you. I know that, but I'm not in the mood.

"Just thought I'd call by to welcome you." Malcolm swayed to keep himself warm.

"We play cards on Thursday," Birdy told me. "You will come won't you? I'm so bored of these people."

Malcolm acted as if he hadn't heard. "It's a lot of fun. We take it in turns to cook dinner and Anwar's doing it this week. He's African so it'll probably be goat. That's what they tend to eat, isn't it?"

He was already getting on my nerves. "Among other things I believe."

"So you'll come?" he tried again.

"The games start at eight sharp." Birdy tipped her hat back to clear a puddle off it. "And dinner's whenever it's ready."

Standing on the top step of the immobile home, looking down at my visitors, I felt like a bouncer in a club. Their names weren't down and they certainly weren't coming in.

"Okay. I'll see you around." I put my hand on the doorframe and Malcolm gave a wet nod then disappeared into the rain-drenched darkness.

"I'm not far if you need anything." Birdy leant to one side to get her message through as I shut her out.

Alone once more, I felt like crying. My clothes were still wet, I'd lost all faith in humanity and I'd just noticed that the caravan had no curtains for some reason.

Try to be positive at least.

This is me trying.

Fine. A sleep might cheer us up?

I got into one of the bunk beds. Ten hours passed. I woke up again feeling just as miserable.

I searched around for something to be happy about and this is what I came up with.

1) **It looked a tiny bit brighter outside than it had the night before – what with it now being daytime.**
2) **I hadn't rolled out of bed and split my head open.**
3) **No tidal waves had lashed the coast overnight, pulling unlucky campers out to sea.**

In a way, it was reassuring. I normally wake up feeling so peppy and cheerful that I forget all about my woes and act as if everything's fine. I needed to sort through my problems, not put them aside and hope for the best.

With a pained sigh, I kicked the duvet off me and took the three steps required to reach the kitchen. I'd brought some supplies from home so I got out of bed and set about crafting the most delicious bacon sandwich known to humankind. Encased within a soft brown hoagie, I added half a bottle of ketchup, melted cheese (controversial choice, I know) slices of pickle, lettuce and a dollop of mango chutney. As I fried up the star ingredient, my brain started singing.

I'm walking on sunshine, whoa-oh!
I'm walking on sunshine, whoa-oh!
And don't it feel good.

Can you believe it? I mean I hadn't come out to the loneliest place I could think of in the worst weather since Noah and his wife decided to take up sailing to be serenaded by peppy eighties pop hits. I'd worked so hard to create a dark, broody atmosphere and just the whiff of bacon had made me feel top of the world again. How was I ever going to sort my life out if I kept being so jolly?

I glued the moody frown back on my face and tried to feel sad that the bacon was taking so long to cook. Looking out through the window, I could see more rain sweeping in on the horizon. Birdy was still outside under her stripy plastic gazebo, reading the paper in the cold. That was sad. Would I end up like her? A lonely septuagenarian forced to find companionship on a campsite with people I could no longer stand?

The bacon had reached prime crispiness so I slung it into my well-adorned bread roll and took a bite.

Oh joy! Oh heavens. It's deserves a Nobel Prize.

Damn you, bacon sandwich. I should have known my funk would be powerless in the light of your earth-shaking deliciousness.

I decided to go outside and chat with my neighbour to see if that would make me feel any worse.

"Morning, Birdy."

"Morning, Isobel." Good start; I hate it when people use my full name.

"Not that it's a particularly cheerful one."

She folded up her newspaper and pointed to the sky. "It says in here that it's only going to get wetter. There's been flooding in Cornwall already. It should be hitting us this afternoon."

YAY! FANTASTIC!

I risked another bite of bacon sandwich, whilst taking careful notice of how tatty her living conditions were. Her caravan looked like she'd found it dumped at the side of the road somewhere. It had large black stains on the door, which I'm pretty sure were burn marks, and one of the windows was badly cracked. How tragic that a woman of her age should be living in such squalid-

Oh my goodness! This sandwich is better than an orgasm.

"You picked a funny time to visit," Birdy continued when I didn't reply. I was probably gurning with pleasure as the exquisite flavours took a tour around my taste buds. "Let me guess, you've come down here for a bit of a mope?"

Ahhhhh! Witch! How did she know?

"Something like that, yeah." I leant against the side of my caravan to escape from the barely visible drizzle that filled the air.

"Due to a member of the less fair sex perhaps?" She rose to standing but stayed beneath the canopy.

"Among other things." I'd liked to have shut this conversation down but that bloody sandwich was firing off endorphins in my brain and making me chatty. "Two blokes in fact. Possibly even three. How did you know?"

"What do you think I'm doing here?" She gave a slow, conspiratorial wink. "I've been married five times, fallen in love a lot more than that and I still can't work out what it's all about. I was seeing a much younger man recently and thought I'd finally found all the answers but it didn't work out."

"When you say *much younger*…"

"He was twenty-seven, my love." That wily minx. "With the mind of Stephen Hawking and the abs of Hugh Jackman. He couldn't handle me though – became too clingy – so I had to cut him loose. This is where I come after a breakup."

So much for the lonely old maid I'd imagined her to be. Birdy was no biddy after all.

"Twenty-seven!" I was struggling to get my head around it. "That's younger than me. Do you have any tips?"

Her face was full of mischief. "I'm afraid not. I've simply never had any problems in that department. There are even men around here who can't resist me. But we've gone off topic, Miss Izzy. Why don't you tell me what's troubling you?"

I'd taken another bite of sandwich and would have run through the details of who killed Bob, my work at Vomeris Hall and almost definitely my credit card pin number. Luckily we were interrupted before I had the chance.

"I'm not happy with you, Birdy." A woman in a plum-coloured tracksuit appeared at the end of the path between our caravans. Her eyes darted in my direction, but she stuck to her task. "You don't respect the bins."

Going by the list that Malcolm had recited the night before, and the fact that she didn't look much like a Mrs Florence Gaskell, I concluded that our new arrival was Debbie from a caravan across the way.

My neighbour rolled her eyes in my direction. "Really, Debs, I only put my stuff out a day early."

"Exactly!" Her voice rocketed to a high note an opera singer would have been proud of. "A whole day for foxes, feral cats and wild boar to come charging through the campsite."

"Debbie, calm down." Birdy tossed her plait over her other shoulder indignantly. "I've never seen feral cats here and I'm pretty sure boar have been extinct in most of Britain for hundreds of years."

"That doesn't change the fact it's a health hazard." Debbie's eyes flashed red. "You should know better at your age!" She got the final phrase out and marched off in the direction she'd come from.

"Cheeky cow." Birdy took a few steps out into the rain to call after her. "You're only seven years younger than me."

"She seemed nice." I didn't try to hide my sarcasm.

"That's Debbie Harrison. Thinks she's the queen of the campsite just because she and her husband have been here longest. You'll soon see that this place is a veritable wasp's nest. Premature rubbish placement is just the beginning."

"I can't wait to meet everyone." I was beginning to like my neighbour but I'd just remembered why my suitcase was so heavy. I made my excuses and went inside.

Here I come, second half of that life-affirming bacon sandwich and a selection from my Agatha Christie library.

An Evening's Entertainment

The '4:50 from Paddington' provided me with all sorts of delights that day. I'd read it about ten times and could more or less remember who the killer was, but it's still nice when I'm not quite sure. I look out for all the clues and it's almost like I'm checking up on whether Dame Agatha did a good enough job. Not that there's much doubt on that score; the woman was a genius.

'4:50 from Paddington' is the one where Miss Marple is too old and feeble to investigate the murder for herself so she sends a surrogate to nose around. Lucy Eyelesbarrow and I had so much in common. We were both capable, young women with shortened first names and multiple gentlemen admirers who we would, at some point, have to choose between. Perhaps the biggest difference I could see was that Lucy had her life together and I was sitting in a very damp caravan on a Thursday afternoon, hiding from the world.

The ridiculous thing about me continuing to read crime fiction was that I had already solved a number of major crimes over the past few months and knew that literary murders weren't much like the real thing. In my experience, killers tend to be more complicated than the outright villain on Christie's train to London. Still, I'd been in Hastings a day and no one had died yet. So that was good.

I was only planning to laze about after lunch but, with the wind and rain attacking the caravan, I struggled to get my head back into the book. The longer I read, the clearer it became that Miss Jane Marple would never have thought of me as a bright young thing like Lucy Eyelesbarrow. She'd have pegged me as one of the not too clever types she's always quick to dismiss.

Lazy, callow, shiftless Izzy Palmer. She reminds me of Marjorie Hemsworth, the butcher's daughter, who ended up in **such** *a terrible state.*

Damn it, Brain! Don't do the Miss Marple voice, you know it freaks me out.

I'd yet to solve any mysteries based on my innate knowledge of character types the way the old maid of St. Mary Mead could and it was making me feel shockingly inferior. So when the evening gloomed by and Birdy knocked on my door, I decided to play cards after all.

"I'd like to tell you it will be heaps of fun, but that would be a lie." She'd barely given me time to grab my anorak and pull my wellies on when she bounded off.

I chased after her over the field to the Welcome Centre, which was shining like a lighthouse through the falling rods of rain.

Birdy walked at an incredible pace, as if she was determined to expend as much energy as possible on the short journey. Her arms swung up to the level of her shoulders and her legs splashed about in the standing water, which was almost as high as the tops of my boots. Beyond the treeline, I could see that the river had burst its banks.

Isn't a house on stilts a good place to be in a flood? I asked myself.

Yeah, but a house fifty miles away from any flooding would be even better.

We took the steps up to the slightly drier patio area in front of our destination and Birdy gave me some final instructions.

"Don't talk to Anwar about his wife, she's forever away on business and he'll keep you chatting all night if you mention her." I could barely hear over the sound of the rain performing a steady drumroll on my hood. "Mrs Florence Gaskell doesn't like it when people mention events that happened after 1977 and we have a sneaking suspicion that Roger is a crossdresser. Got that?"

She wrenched the door open and we paraded into the steamy glass box that functioned as the campsite's reception, social centre and café. The large, brightly lit space had a bank of photos of past summer visitors on one wall and the rest of the room was white and featureless. Several tables were set out, but only the one in the centre of the room was occupied. We were the last to arrive.

"My dear child." An incredibly ancient-looking woman in a rather grand armchair extended a skinny hand in my direction. "I've been dying to meet you." She wore a fur-trimmed cardigan and had a peacock feather fascinator in her hair.

"Mrs Florence Gaskell," Birdy and I whispered at the same time, as we made our way over.

She was sitting at the end of a trestle table with the other residents spread around it. To complement her Queen-like attire, she held an ornate walking stick in one hand like it was her sceptre. I was unable to resist the magnetic weirdness that she exuded.

"My name," she paused for effect as if she was about to say Elizabeth Taylor or Beyoncé, "is Mrs Florence Gaskell. No doubt you've heard of me."

"It's lovely to meet you."

"Here you go, Izzy." Birdy handed me a can of beer. "That should help the evening go smoother."

"Izzy? Hello, Izzy?" Through a process of elimination I knew the short man who popped up from the table beside me was Roger. He had a slight, unassuming presence and was wearing a matching purple tracksuit to his wife's.

"Hello, Roger." I didn't know where to go from there.

"You know my name?" This made him happy. "How lovely." He had a very compacted look to him, like someone had put him through one of those machines for crushing cars. He was such an insubstantial man and contrasted perfectly with the old lady beside him. I thought perhaps that, if I turned my head, he'd disappear.

The duchess of the campsite hadn't finished and grabbed my free arm to wrestle me into the seat next to hers. She was a lot stronger than she looked. "Sit next to me, dear child. I'll tell you all my secrets."

Birdy settled down opposite. "She means she'll look at your cards during the game. Won't you, Flo?"

Florence took exception to this accusation and turned her gaze from her neighbour to look out at the rain. "I don't remember weather like this since 1953!"

Birdy winked at me across the table.

"So, what is that you do, Izzy?" Whilst removing a deck of cards from their box, Debbie launched the question at me like it was an insult. She had a rusty brown tan that smacked more of sunbed than sunshine.

"I'm sort of between jobs at the moment."

"Oh, unemployed you mean?" The multitude of lines around her eyes creased up gleefully as she spoke. "You should get yourself down to a job centre instead of hanging out here."

"Darling-" Roger began but his wife ignored him.

She hadn't made a great second impression and I was happy to set

17

her straight. "Actually, I've just finished up a job in finance and I've got some seed money for a company of my own." It was mostly true.

"That sounds impressive, doesn't it?" Roger beamed across the table and his wife's dried-up face shrivelled in disappointment.

Just then a large, jolly-looking man who I hadn't seen before rolled out of the kitchen with a bowl of salad in his hand.

"Alright, mate? I'm Anwar." He put the bowl down on the table and his hand on my shoulder. "You probably guessed that though as I'm the only one around here with a bit of colour!" He gave a big echoing laugh at his own joke then spotted Debbie's unimpressed expression. "Hey, no offence, Debs!"

Birdy joined in with his laughter and I could see where the battle lines lay in this bizarre little community of retirees.

"Is it goat we're having for dinner?" Malcolm asked from the other end of the table.

Despite all I'd heard about Anwar's heritage, every word he spoke was coated in a cockney accent. "What you on about, Mal?"

"For dinner." Malcolm was entirely serious. "That's what you eat in Africa, isn't it?"

"What? You think all people eat over a whole continent is goat? I ain't making flipping goat. We're having rigatoni." Another big laugh. "Don't mind Malcolm, Izzy. He's not actually a racist, he just sounds like one."

"Are we playing cards or talking politics?" Mrs Florence Gaskell asked, looking deeply offended that Anwar had used the r word.

We had a couple of hands of poker before dinner and I realised that I was way out of my depth. Mrs Gaskell's little-old-lady demeanour disappeared as soon as the cards had been dealt. She played like a Vegas shark and I was glad of the break when dinner was served.

The end of the table where the married couple were sitting remained uncomfortably quiet, but Birdy made sure that I was entertained. "Tell Izzy your claim to fame, Flo."

A cheeky smile occupied Florence's face. "Have you heard of the O'Driscoll scandal in the sixties?"

It rang a bell. "Something to do with a politician, wasn't it?"

"That's right." She gave me an affectionate poke on the arm. "Well I was Lord O'Driscoll's secret mistress. I almost brought down the government."

"How about someone comes up with a different story?" Malcolm suggested.

"Don't be so dull, Malcolm." Birdy sounded quite angry at this. "You know that Mrs Florence Gaskell has all the best ones."

"This is delicious," I told our chef, to lighten the mood. "Did you make it yourself?"

"Oh yes, we all know what a great cook Anwar is!" Debbie cast her fork down on the table with a clatter. "We have to put up with the smell of his kitchen being pumped into our bedroom night after night."

Anwar was immediately on his feet. "Hey, it's not my fault that the extractor fan is on your side of the plot. What do you want me to do? Go hungry?"

"Roger, are you going to let him talk to me like that?" Debbie looked at her husband as if he was the one who'd offended her.

There was a moment of stillness before Roger's quiet reply. "Why don't we all calm down and play some cards?"

"Why don't you stick up for your wife?" Birdy hurled the words across at the nondescript man in the terrible tracksuit. He was more like a sketch of a human than an actual person.

Somehow, the old lady and I were the only ones who weren't afire with anger right then. Anwar was furiously forking pasta into his mouth, with his eyes locked onto his neighbour. Debbie herself was jabbing her husband with her pointy elbow. Malcolm had put his hands to his head and was pulling at his curly locks and Birdy was giving poor Roger a lecture on what a terrible decision he'd made ever getting married.

I looked at Mrs Florence Gaskell to see what she made of the whole thing but she didn't seem particularly worried.

"It happens about once a month," she told me. "They're just blowing off steam. It will all calm down before long."

She was right in one way because, ten seconds later, just as Debbie was about to chuck her plate across the table, there was an enormous crash that reduced everyone to silence.

"It's the skylight in the kitchen," Malcolm shouted, giving up on his self-punishment to leap from his seat. "The rain must be getting in."

With the exception of the grande dame of Hastings' Caravan Park, we all followed after him into the neighbouring room. The floor was already flooded and gallons of water were pouring in from the flat roof above the kitchen.

Anwar sprang into action, giving out commands to everyone. He was surprisingly swift on his feet, despite the water he had to wade through. "Debbie, grab the mop and broom from the cupboard. Birdy get the little step ladder from outside. Roger, we're going to need the wooden board from beside my caravan and you'll have to find a hammer and some nails from the storeroom while you're at it."

"Anything I can do?" I thought I should at least try to be helpful.

Anwar was searching through the cupboards for two large bowls and, on finding them, handed one to me. "You've got the most important job of all."

The water was freezing as it splashed down through the cracked glass. My arms soon got tired and I kept wobbling and tipping the bowl so that my body turned to ice. Whenever it was full, I handed it down to Debbie who swapped it for an empty one. I was the only person tall enough to hold it there. Thinking about it now, I'm pretty sure it would have been enough to put an empty bin on the floor under the hole, but it seemed like the right idea at the time.

Anwar and Malcolm had climbed up onto the roof and I could hear them sweeping the water off to be able to board up the broken window.

Five minutes later it was all done and everyone seemed very happy with themselves as we dried off in the café area.

"I think it's about time we opened a bottle of wine," Florence said and the rest of us cheered with approval.

"Better make it champagne." Anwar emerged from the kitchen with a bottle in his hand. "Well Prosecco, but it's the same thing, isn't it?"

Debbie didn't look as though she agreed but kept her mouth shut. I was amazed how we'd gone from all-out warfare to cheery cordiality in such a short space of time.

They were all completely mad and I loved it.

Afterhours

I should have known to quit the game as soon as someone mentioned playing for money. Mrs Florence Gaskell could have been on one of those late-night poker shows and I was broke within the hour. I'm just glad I hadn't brought any valuables with me. She'd have had Mum's car key off me next.

Birdy fared far better than I did and seemed to be able to read her fellow residents' expressions instinctively.

"Fifty quid is all the sweeter when I get to prise it from their miserable hands." She told me when it was time to return to our side of the caravan park and we'd dropped Florence off. She didn't have much sympathy for my lighter wallet.

"What's up with you all? Why do you keep coming here if you hate each other?"

Perhaps they're sadists? Perhaps they're swingers!
Shhh!!

The rain was coming down just as heavily as before and the water was up to our knees now. If it got much higher, we'd have to evacuate.

"Long story, my love. Fancy a nightcap and I'll fill you in on all the juicy details?"

How could I resist such an offer? My desire for solitude was all but forgotten and I was hypnotised by this hotbed of middle-class eccentricity.

The inside of Birdy's caravan was just as drab and worn looking as the exterior. The walls were covered in swirly yellow wallpaper from the seventies and the furniture looked like it would break if you touched it. Being there made me feel rather sad for her again, despite the fact she was the toughest woman I'd ever met.

"Whiskey?" Of course she drank whiskey and the fact she served it up in chipped Christmas mugs made it all the cooler. I couldn't stand the stuff and would much rather have had a lemonade or a nice hot chocolate, but I pretended to enjoy it.

Before she got started on local gossip, she filled me in on her career as an apparently ground-breaking chemist. "There's a plastic alloy I developed which bears my name. If I'm being honest my second husband worked on it too, and got far too much of the credit, but I was the one who landed on the exact formula."

I just sat there and listened as she regaled me with stories of her fascinating life and unique perspective on the world. She was so confident about everything and it made me wish I could be more like her. She made bold, beautiful statements like, "The only reason humans were put on this planet was to evolve, develop new technologies and find a way off it." She was quickly becoming my hero.

"Can I let you into a secret?" she asked, untying her long silver hair so that she could casually run her hands through it as she sat looking at me in the dim light.

I nodded, though I'm pretty sure she would have told me anyway.

"I believe in magic." She laughed at her own words and I realised that this wasn't the first time she'd said them. "I know it's ridiculous for a scientist to say, but it's true. There are so many things which defy explanation and I'm one of them. You see, ever since I was a little girl, I've found that people have been drawn to me. I don't think it's because of how I look or my personality, and you could put it down to pheromones or something along those lines, but I believe it's more than that.

"I can think of no other reason why my sexy young ex became so obsessed with me, or why my fourth husband threatened to jump out of a window if I left him. It's not always romantic either. It happens just as much with women as men and I have close friends who've attempted to explain it without ever landing on the words."

I took a sip of the bitter liquid she'd given me. "Are you serious?"

"Quite, my love. How else can you explain why you're sitting in the world's ugliest caravan at almost midnight with an old lady you hardly know?" As she said the words, my presence there came into focus. I suddenly felt out of place.

"You really mean it, don't you?"

She made a face like I was a child asking a silly question. "Of course. Isn't there anything about yourself you can't explain?"

A new feeling zoomed up within me and I desperately wanted her respect. I had the urge to tell her about the murders I'd investigated and how I'd been the only one capable of identifying the killers. By the time I'd asked myself why I cared what she thought, the conversation had already moved on.

"You know, around the time I first started coming here, I made an effort to be thoroughly objectionable." Her sparkling silver eyes glowed in the darkness and I again imagined she was some kind of witch. "I was rude to everyone I met and took great pleasure in being disruptive and confrontational. It didn't work though. For the most part, people found me just as charming as ever.

"There are always exceptions. Debbie for one has never been receptive to me but, if anything, that simply reinforces my belief. If it's my special power to attract those around me, it stands to reason that there are those who have the ability to resist. As a scientist, I'd like to believe it's some kind of force we haven't found a name for yet, just as hundreds of years ago, people didn't understand gravity."

I couldn't tell if she was making a confession, or trying to show off. She straightened up in her chair and it felt as if she'd released me from a spell.

"You were going to tell me about the other residents here," I said, feeling strangely keen to change the topic.

Her face hardened for a second and I could see that she was sizing me up. She relaxed once more and it was clear that she would let me escape from her strange little world of hypnotic powers and besotted admirers.

"Where should I start?" She took a good slug of whiskey then answered her own question. "Anwar is a phenomenon in himself. Chirpy and loveable but with a temper to bulldoze a factory; you don't want to get on the wrong side of him – as Roger and Debbie have discovered a number of times.

"Malcolm is an odd one. He's a sort of benign busybody. He finds out all sorts of nasty things about everyone but chooses not to use them against us. It seems his greatest wish is to be a good campsite manager and, as long as we're happy, he's tickety-boo."

"What about Mrs Florence Gaskell?" I stood up from my lumpy armchair to look out at the never-ending storm before settling back down on the broad wooden windowsill.

"Old Florence, isn't who she says she is." Running her fingers up and down the handle of her whiskey mug, I could tell that Birdy was trying to decide whether I deserved the truth. "But what she doesn't realise is that the fake she's been her whole life is far more interesting than the people she's claimed to be."

"You mean she's a con woman?"

She leant forward in her chair. "No, she was a con woman. Now she's a charming old lady who's enjoying her retirement. She told me a while back that the real Florence Gaskell died years ago and I'm pretty sure I'm the only person here who knows it. In our way, we're quite close. Florence likes to tell people that she can afford to live here because of an allowance the O'Driscoll family pay her for not testifying to the affair. The truth is that she's penniless and I'm the one supporting her."

By this point, my drink was empty but I pretended to sip from it so that Birdy wouldn't offer me any more. "That's nice of you."

"Not really, my love. She's not the only one with secrets to keep."

"And Debbie and Roger?"

Birdy went to grab the whiskey bottle from the Formica table in front of her but then changed her mind. "I find them the most interesting of the lot. If Debbie and I weren't such great enemies, I think we'd make wonderful friends – though I doubt Roger would be very happy about it."

Every word she said surprised me. "Why do you say that?"

"They're two of the most normal people I've ever met. I find them to be the perfect representatives of our incredible country. They are open and accepting, kind-hearted and generous but strangely terrified of the outside world. In my way, I rather love them. Plus they have the most fantastically dreadful fashion-sense of anyone in Sussex, which I think is marvellous."

She had a wistful look on her face as she stood up, took my mug from me and dumped it into the sink. "Now, if you've no more questions, my love, I'm afraid I'm a little tired."

"Of course." I jumped down from my perch and moved towards the door as she delivered her parting piece of wisdom.

"I'm a bit like Cinderella, you know. By the time it gets to midnight, the illusion shatters."

"I'll see you for breakfast."

She held my gaze for a moment and I thought she would speak again. When she didn't, I descended the steps from her caravan and went out into the storm.

A Corpse in a Caravan

I didn't sleep well that night. The wind marauding through the trees sounded like someone crying out in pain. When I managed to fall asleep, my dreams were lurid and violent. At one point I was being murdered on a train, later on, I was dead in a ditch, sentient but unable to move. And that was nothing compared to the long passages where I was simply drinking tea in a chintzy sitting room with an old lady who didn't think much of my manners. It was a very British sort of nightmare.

Even when I stirred and then fell back to sleep, I couldn't shake off the bad dreams. The sitting room was soon filled with ex-boyfriends and current loves. There was seventeen-year-old Gary Flint pouring Miss Marple her tea. Standing just behind them was Danny, my childhood crush, and peering through the window, begging to come in, was a shady figure. I knew instantly that it was the man I loved most in the world, who I had left nice dry Croydon to try find some headspace away from.

At one point my teacher from nursery school dropped by too, and for some reason my clothes were covered in milk. I woke up early and lay in bed watching the sky.

Why doesn't this caravan have any bloody curtains!?

It had stopped raining for the first time in days but the wind was still howling about, gently rocking the box I was living in.

I remembered what Birdy had told me about her magnetic powers the night before and I wasn't sure I believed her. I wasn't sure her bizarre idea was even a serious suggestion. And yet, what I wanted more than anything right then was to get out of bed, wrap myself up in a dressing gown and continue our conversation over breakfast. What else could explain the pull that I was feeling? Either everything she'd told me was true or she was a sophisticated manipulator who had planted the idea in my head. I was looking forward to finding out which it was.

I didn't jump out into the swampy field to discover the truth though. I took my time over breakfast, made myself a hot chocolate with the milk all frothy and delicious and then, cool and casually, wandered out.

The water had subsided a little. It never reached as high as the static caravan doors and none of the mobile homes had floated away in the night. It all felt oddly disappointing, like an unfulfilled promise.

There was no sign of Birdy. Her stripy plastic gazebo resembled an unattended sentry box. The campsite was dead except for Malcolm who, dressed in waist-high waders, was making his way around to check for flood damage.

"Morning. Have you seen Birdy today?" I asked when he got to the caravans opposite mine.

"Good morning, Izzy." He didn't stop moving but kept peering through the boarded-up windows of the unattended units. "I'd have seen her if she'd gone out. Have you knocked?"

I took it as a rhetorical question and descended into the freezing water to make the brief journey over to my neighbour. Birdy's curtains were still drawn and they were too high up to look through even for me. I climbed the fold-down steps and knocked on her door. No sound came back so I tried again. The smiley-faced watch that my mum had given me for my fifteenth birthday told me that it was ten to nine. I would probably have given up and assumed she was still asleep, but then Malcolm reappeared from his task.

"She's an early riser, there's no way she'd be sleeping until now. I'd better check it out."

Rather him than me, I thought, imagining the anger Birdy would direct at him if she emerged prematurely from the bathroom.

He knocked once more and then tried the handle, which resisted for a second before giving way. Pulling the door open, a sudden rush of water sent him flying backwards. Birdy's caravan was flooded. Malcolm fell from the steps, knocking into me, and the force of the water carried us both to the open space between the rows of mobile homes.

Malcolm shot his arm down to steady himself and ended up pushing me under the water. It was only a few seconds but I lost my orientation and my head dragged down with the rest of my body so that I came up coughing and choking.

"Are you okay?" He asked, sloshing over to help me up and smack me on the back.

I didn't answer. As soon as I'd caught my breath, I shot off towards

Birdy's caravan where the water was still flooding out. I pulled myself up using the handles on either side of the door.

"Call the police, an ambulance too maybe," I shouted back to Malcolm before I ducked through. "My phone's in the caravan if you need it."

Inside, the water was up to my waist but I could see that it had been higher. The sunroof was agape and a tap had been left on in the sink. Every cupboard and drawer had come open, so a mess of kitchen utensils, clothes and toiletries clogged up the space as I fought my way through. It took me a moment to realise that, over by the dining area where we'd sat to talk the night before, Birdy was floating face down.

She was a big woman and her clothes were soaking, so lifting her out of the water felt like a tug-of-war. Her loose silver hair stuck to her face as I held her under the arms in the vain hope that she might still be alive. Her eyes were closed but I guess the cold water had prevented much decay of the body as she looked much the same as when I'd left her there, hours before. Well, that's not true. She looked cold, frightened even, but not rotting and gross.

Malcolm appeared in the doorway, my phone to his ear. He looked over at me with a question on his lips that would never be spoken.

"You can cancel the ambulance," I told him, straining not to drop Birdy's body back into the water. "She's dead."

The police arrived ten minutes later. It was almost comical to sit out on my steps and watch them slowly make their way over to us. They didn't have waders or even high boots and I could see they were soon just as cold as I had been. Most of the water had drained out of Birdy's caravan by the time they got there and a couple of younger officers were required to search around the campsite looking for any important evidence that had been washed away. They retrieved stockings and frying pans, a kitchen knife and a bunch of sodden books.

When they were finished, their senior officer directed them to interview the residents. An extremely nervous woman came into my caravan and sipped at the tea I made us both as she asked me questions. I told her everything that had happened since I'd arrived and she carefully noted it down.

I watched from my porch as the other residents emerged from their homes. Debbie was the only one who cried, which I found kind of sad and wonderful. Perhaps Birdy's nemesis was the one who'd miss her most. It didn't last long though. She went back to shouting at Anwar as soon as the police had moved on.

"Course any forensic evidence will have been washed away," an overly chatty inspector called D.I. Stone informed me when they appeared to be winding up their inquiries. Going by the tight-lipped officers I'd known back home, I wasn't convinced he had the discretion to make it in the Metropolitan Police Force.

I looked down at him from the decking. "So you're treating it as a crime then?"

He was a short, tubby man with a permanently unimpressed face. "Not really. Classic suicide, I reckon. Taps left on is always a sign. It's like she wanted to wash away any trace of herself."

I was having trouble making sense of what had happened. "Are you saying she didn't drown?"

"No, love. Wrists were slit. Didn't you see?"

I already didn't like him. "That doesn't sound anything like the woman I knew."

He pulled a damp pad of paper out of his top pocket and flipped through it. "You told one of my officers that you'd only met her a couple of days ago." In an instant, his tone turned from idle and breezy to outright stern. "Doesn't sound like you're in much of a position to be contradicting me now, does it?"

He was wrong, so I ignored him. I wondered for a moment how many murder investigations a small-town police officer would have seen in his career. I was on my third already and I'd only been an accidental detective for a few months.

Not that we're cocky or anything.

No. Of course not.

"We appreciate you helping us with our enquiries." His voice softened again and I felt a bit guilty for judging him so harshly. "We'll get the post mortem results back in a few days and then we'll know for sure."

I couldn't stop thinking about the state Birdy had been in when I found her. Hers wasn't the first dead body I'd seen but the others had been different. I hadn't particularly liked them for one thing and I hadn't had to pull them out of a flood. The memory of that moment would never leave me.

I stayed in my caravan that whole day. I didn't feel like eating because there was the corpse of a nice old lady dancing through my head and the two didn't go together. I couldn't read my book either because I was tired of death.

I felt just as frozen as when I'd emerged from the waters of our flooded field so I wrapped myself up in my blanket and sat in front of a portable heater. Even this couldn't melt away the cold that had penetrated deep inside. With my feet almost burning against the red hot grill, I tried to clear my mind.

Malcolm came to see me that afternoon.

"We'll be going ahead with our regular Friday activity this evening, it's what Birdy would have wanted."

"What do you do on Fridays?" I asked.

He was hovering in the doorway in his usual hesitant manner. "Quiz night and hotdogs. It's what Birdy would have wanted." He was evidently trying to convince himself that this was the case.

"I don't think I'll be coming, sorry." I hadn't moved from my cosy spot on the sofa. "And I'll probably head home tomorrow."

"But you were supposed to be here a whole week." My change of plan didn't fit into his neatly organised view of the world. "The others will be sad."

I should probably have packed up right then and made my way back to Croydon. It seemed like death was following me wherever I went and I didn't want to see another of the nice old residents of Hastings Caravan Park bumped off.

The longer I sat there in my toasty chrysalis, the harder it was for me to believe that Birdy had killed herself. I'd known depressed people before. A girl in my flat in uni had tried to take an overdose, Birdy was nothing like that. She was full of unfulfilled ambitions and half-completed plans. Why would she have chosen that night to kill herself? Why flood her own caravan? Nothing added up.

As no one else was trying to make sense of what had happened, it looked like it would be down to me to work it out.

Just a Friendly Chat

At eight o'clock, I was already there helping Malcolm with the hot dogs.

"That's what I like to call community spirit," he said when Debbie and Roger arrived, looking surprised to see me.

"I just didn't want to be alone in the caravan any longer." I kept my eyes on the tubes of pinky-brown meat bobbing up and down in the boiling water.

"Ahh, it must have been terrible for you, darling."

That's right, Debbie. And yet you're the one who cried. Why was that?

"I mean, I know she and I didn't get on, but I wouldn't have wished what happened to her on anyone." Her tan looked all the brighter in the gloom of the dingy kitchen. Roger stood behind his wife, grinning inanely and occasionally humming in agreement.

I'd already transported the fake Mrs Florence Gaskell to her usual place which meant only Anwar was still to join us. He showed up five minutes after we'd sat down to eat, full of his usual pep.

"This is bloody delicious, Izzy. Nobody told me you were a chef."

"It's only a hotdog." Malcolm had failed to grasp Anwar's sarcasm.

"I know, Mal. That's why it's funny."

"It's an old family recipe." I gave Malcolm a teasing nudge so that he could feel included in our joke. "Been passed down through the generations. The secret is to heat the frankfurters before you eat them."

"Wow. I'd never have thought of that." Anwar's great big laugh reverberated around the room but came to a sudden halt as Debbie lost her cool.

"I don't know what you're all so happy about at a time like this." Her mouth and nose squished in together in the middle of her face. She looked like she was daring us to shout back at her.

No one took the bait. Florence began to whistle a happy tune and, with the last bite of his bread roll poked into his mouth, Malcolm stood up to play peacemaker.

"Okay everybody. Why don't we start the quiz?" As there were no objections, he grabbed a box of trivia questions down from a shelf. "Anwar and Debbie can be team captains and I'll have the final decision in the event of any disagreements. Mrs Florence Gaskell will be our timekeeper."

The old lady smiled and brandished a stopwatch. It appeared her role was more ceremonial than anything as there was no particular time limit set for the questions. The rival captains eyed one another from opposite sides of the table. Roger and I would be dragged along with them to wherever this particular confrontation was headed.

"History round. Question number one." Malcolm paused, his gaze flicking between the two teams. "Who is the only British king to be beheaded for treason?"

Debbie was the first to reply. "Henry the Somethingth!?"

Malcolm allowed a second of tension before answering. "That's not what I have written here. I'm going to throw it over to Anwar and Izzy."

We looked at each other and Anwar signalled for me to try. "Charles the First?"

"That is correct. One point to the A-team!"

And Dad said that choosing history at school would never be useful. Thank you, Mrs Long!

"Question number two. Name one of the princes who died mysteriously in the Tower of London?"

"Edward," Roger piped up. "Bound to be. Most royals back then were called Edward."

"You stupid little man." Debbie was not happy with her husband's reasoning. "I'm the team captain. All decisions should go through me."

Malcolm looked uncertain what to do. "Would you like to change your mind?"

"Ahem." Florence cleared her throat theatrically. "I'm not sure that's allowed."

"Yes, I would," Debbie said, ignoring the complaint. "I'll go with William."

"Final answer?" Malcolm demanded.

"Yes, final answer!"

He made an over-the-top sad expression. "I'm afraid that is incorrect. A-Team?"

Anwar thought for a second but I knew exactly what he would say. "How about Edward?"

Our quizmaster pointed his finger decisively. "Correct! Edward and Richard were the two princes in the tower."

It was Roger who gave the biggest cheer and his wife who reacted. "We didn't get the point, you fool."

"Which shows you should trust your husband more." Roger's smile hadn't disappeared and I was afraid that Debbie might do something about it.

Malcolm moved us swiftly on. "Question number three. What was the name of the deranged fan who shot and killed John Lennon in New York in 1980?"

"Is every question going to be about murder?" Florence asked. "It's not really the day for that."

Anwar put his hand on the old lady's shoulder. "It's just a coincidence, Flo. And anyway, Birdy wasn't murdered."

"Yes she was."

The room fell silent. No one made a sound as their eyes fell on me.

"Why would you say that?" Anwar was glaring as if I was the killer.

"Because it's true." I took a moment to watch their reaction. "And I'm pretty sure one of you did it."

The room erupted in a bonfire of shock and recriminations as they all talked over one another.

"There's something not right with that one!" Roger pointed at me with one very poky finger.

"Who would think up with something like that?" Debbie asked, but, for once, hers wasn't the angriest response.

Malcolm had thrown a handful of question cards into the air and they fluttered down around us like leaves in autumn. "This is supposed to be a quiz night. It's supposed to be fun! Why does everything around here end up so dark and miserable?"

Silence once more reigned in the Hastings Caravan Park Welcome Centre. Malcolm's outburst had seemingly outdone my revelation in the drama stakes and I was momentarily forgotten.

"Here, Mal." Anwar got up to guide him to a chair. "Have a seat and you'll feel better."

"I just want everyone to have a nice time." Our manager was practically in tears.

"Listen, girl." Debbie fixed me with her gaze. "Why would you accuse us of being murderers out of the blue like that?"

I made them sweat for a few more ticks of the faded, green wall clock. "Birdy and I had a long conversation in her caravan last night. She was in a great mood and told me all sorts of things. She was proud of her achievements and happy with her lifestyle. There's no way she'd have killed herself."

"You hardly knew her," Roger said, his voice stuttering. "Why should we listen to you?"

"That's right. Maybe Birdy was depressed or something." Anwar leant on the table, his head resting on one hand. "It's not always obvious what someone's feeling deep down."

I kept my emotions under control. "I'm telling you now that, when the post-mortem results come back in a few days, there'll be a bruise on her head somewhere, or drugs in her system, because there's no chance in hell that she slit her own wrists."

"Why should we listen to you?" Debbie was next up to challenge me. "Where's your evidence?"

"There isn't any because it got conveniently washed away." I may have overplayed the drama here, my voice went all breathy and mysterious. "Obviously, whoever opened Birdy's sunroof got the idea when the skylight in the kitchen crashed in."

Angry responses once more rung out around me but they were silenced by an unexpected voice.

"I believe you, Izzy." Mrs Florence Gaskell stretched one elegant hand along the table for me to hold. "I'm sure that Birdy would never have taken her own life, and I can't imagine anyone else coming down here in this weather."

Anwar looked around at his fellow residents, as if seeing them in a different light. "I didn't bloody do it."

"Well, that's easy to say." Debbie brought the flat of her hand down onto the table in front of her. "We all had our issues with the old bag."

Anwar didn't like the sound of that. "Oh yeah, so what's mine then?"

"She used to make fun of you. Thought you were a bit thick. It was obvious that she got under your skin every time she spoke."

Anwar snapped right back. "No one likes being talked down to, mate. Doesn't mean I killed her."

Debbie straightened up in her seat, a knowing smile on her creased-paper face. "Yeah, but this was more than that, wasn't it? Ever since you arrived here, you've been looking for a way to show her what you're really made of."

"You're talking rubbish." He ran both hands through his thinning hair.

"Is that what happened? Did you go over to the caravan to tell Birdy what you thought of her? Did it get out of hand so you had to cover your tracks?"

This was incredible. Even better than I'd hoped. They were doing my job for me.

Anwar took a breath, slowed it all down. He held back his words until he was sure they were the right ones. "You've got a great imagination, Debs, but that doesn't make me the killer. Anyway, if we're picking a suspect based on who Birdy bumped heads with, then I know who my money's on."

I liked his style. He'd turned the tables and suddenly Debbie was the one on the defensive.

"I beg your pardon?"

I thought that Malcolm would stay out of the whole discussion but he had his own piece to say. "Oh, come on, Debbie. You can't deny it. You hated her with a passion."

Even Roger was staring at his wife, anticipating how she would respond.

"I'm not going to suggest that we were best friends or say how great she was, just because she's popped her clogs, but-"

There was something missing and I had to interrupt. "Hold that thought." I nipped into the kitchen, grabbed a pack of beer from the fridge and returned to hand them out. "Go on with what you were saying."

Debbie cracked one of the large cans open and resumed her argument. "No, I didn't like Birdy. She was selfish and untidy. She didn't care about rules and she thought she could take whatever she wanted, even when it wasn't hers."

"Don't forget the bins," Roger added.

"Oh, the bins. If I'd told her once, I'd told her a thousand times. She always put her bin out the night before and I swear I saw a rat once."

"Though it might have been a sparrow."

"Yes, thank you, Roger. It might have been a sparrow." The married couple had been together so long that they had the same cascading rhythm to their sentences. "Birdy wasn't the angel that she made out, but I like to think we respected one another."

I'd been watching her the whole time she spoke but she caught my eye then and I guess I failed to hide a smile.

"What?" She pulled her arms across her chest like I'd thrown something at her. "What is it, Izzy?"

I tried really hard to keep a straight face. "It's just…" A full-on giggle escaped my lips. "You cried. When you found out that Birdy was dead, you started crying."

Debbie glanced about uncomfortably. "Yeah, well obviously I was… I mean… if one person gets killed, it's more likely that another will. And then…" She swallowed her jumbled words back down. "I could be next."

That's it. We've got her.

Oh, totally. She should have just said she was shocked to hear the news, but instead she lied. She hadn't been expecting my question so she wasn't prepared and her guilt shone through. No doubt about it.

Debbie Harrison, you're going down.

"Who's to say it was one of us?" Perhaps sensing that his wife was on unsteady ground, Roger was up next. "What about that young fella she was seeing?"

"What young fella?" Anwar sounded relieved to be out of the spotlight.

"She was dating some bloke in his twenties from the university she used to work at." The whole time he was speaking, Roger played with the zip on his sea-green tracksuit top. He opened and closed it, over and over. "They broke up not so long ago. What's to say that he didn't drive down here, murder his lover and smash the sunroof to hide the evidence?"

"It wasn't smashed," Malcolm corrected him. "The killer just opened it to let the rain in."

"Whatever. My point is, there's nothing to say that it was one of us. If there even was a killer, which I'm still not convinced about." Roger was getting really worked-up. "Let's forget all this pointless speculation."

"No, let's keep going." Malcolm sounded oddly determined. "Debbie says it wasn't her. Fine. Who's next?"

"Roger," I decided for the group. "No one's above suspicion."

"Why would I have killed Birdy?" His voice got all high and reedy as the attention remained with him.

"To stand up for your wife?" I guess this was Anwar's version of revenge for what Debbie had just put him through. "Maybe you didn't like the way that Birdy answered back to the two of you. Maybe it was time someone taught her a lesson."

Normally I'd be the one stringing together theories and interrogating my suspects until one of them cracked. For the first time that week, I felt like I was on a real holiday.

Now if only we could do something about the weather.

"Well, that's just brilliant." Roger took a swig of beer. "You're the reincarnation of Sherlock Holmes."

Anwar cocked his head back and very pointedly announced, "Sherlock Holmes wasn't real!"

"I know that, thank you, Anwar. And neither is reincarnation."

"The parking space." Malcolm was suddenly animated again and began to gesture about as he spoke. "You wanted an extra parking space next to Debbie's but you couldn't have one because Birdy's space was in the way. You were furious when I gave you the bad news. I've never seen anyone go from calm to outright steaming so quickly. You were like a bomb going off."

His eyebrows raised to the heavens, Roger looked genuinely offended. "Are you seriously suggesting that I'd kill someone for the sake of a parking space?"

"Yes, I am!"

"That's exactly what you'd say if you wanted to shift the blame." Roger looked happy with himself to have reached this conclusion.

"I have nothing to hide." Malcolm's burst of energy had subsided.

It was quiet for a moment until Florence started to laugh. "Oh come along, dear boy. We all know about your eccentricities."

Slumping in his chair, Malcolm looked less certain than he had a moment earlier. "What do you mean?"

The grand old lady gripped her amethyst-topped cane and smiled. "You dress up as a woman to every costume party we put on. Mrs Claus for our Christmas do, a zombie Marilyn Monroe for Halloween. You even went as Jessica Rabbit for the Easter parade."

"I was just entering into the spirit of things." His eyes darting frantically about, Malcolm looked like a boxed-in weasel. "And what does it have to do with Birdy's death?"

Debbie spoke under her breath but made sure that everyone could hear. "Perhaps she caught you dressing up in her stockings and you didn't want her telling everyone."

"That's enough." I intervened at last. After all, I already knew who the killer was. I didn't want anyone getting upset unnecessarily. "Malcolm's private habits have got nothing to do with Birdy's death."

Anwar turned to Malcolm with a smile on his face, as if he'd been absent for the rest of the conversation. "To be honest, Mal, I always wondered if you had a little crush on Birdy. You seemed to sort of admire her somehow."

After the noise and commotion that had roared around the plain white room for so long, a tense calm descended.

Malcolm had lost his confidence entirely and stared down at the floor. "If we're being honest, I don't think I've ever had a crush on anyone in my entire life. I don't know what it is about me, but love isn't an emotion I appear to be capable of."

Anwar looked at Mrs Florence Gaskell to know what to do and when she didn't suggest anything, he patted Malcolm on the arm and said, "Don't be so hard on yourself. I can't roll my tongue if it makes you feel any better."

"I always thought I'd find someone in the end but it wasn't to be." Even Debbie and Roger looked sad for him. "Don't feel sorry for me, I'm perfectly happy here with you lot. That's why I try so hard to make sure you're having a good time."

Florence was the only one still smiling. A brief light had been shone on the reality of their lives there and they settled into quiet reflection. Anwar looked out at the dark field beyond the windows and twiddled his wedding ring round and round on his finger.

"What about me?" Mrs Florence Gaskell asked her ruminant neighbours. "Perhaps I killed Birdy. Is it really so hard to believe?"

Finally looking up from the speckled white floor, Malcolm was the first to reply. "You'd never do that Mrs G."

"Oh? Why are you so sure?" From her throne at the end of the table, she peered around at us.

No one answered at first. Perhaps we felt uncomfortable drawing attention to the physical element of the murder that would surely have been beyond her. We left the talking to Malcolm.

"What possible reason would you have?"

"Exactly. Not one of you can think of a reason. None of you know much about me in fact, but Birdy did. She knew all my secrets. Perhaps I did the deed to stop her spilling them." There was already something magical about this great lady of Hastings and, with her smile stretched wide across her face, she looked like the Cheshire Cat.

"Did you?" Anwar fought to get the two short words out.

"No, my dear child. I did not. But I don't like to be overlooked."

The tension in the room broke and her smile spread around the table.

"So none of us are guilty then," Malcolm exclaimed. "Birdy's death was an unfortunate accident or rather…"

Debbie directed her fiery gaze back in my direction. "Unless this girl was behind it the whole time. After all, she sounded very sure it was a murder."

"What do we even know about her?" Roger was happy to back up his wife's theory. "Coming here and throwing her accusations around. Who even is she?"

Malcolm was quick to address any administrative issues. "She's Danny's friend. He rang to say she'd be coming."

"Oh, yeah?" Roger crushed his empty can in one hand. "And did he send a photo? Did he tell you what this friend looked like? Perhaps the woman in front of us is an imposter and the real Izzy is dead in her car."

"Do you wanna see my driving licence?" I suggested. "That should clear things up."

This ignited a buzz of chatter which was soon cut short by Florence's intervention.

"Let's not get carried away. Izzy isn't the killer either. Though I imagine she's something of a theatre lover. Isn't that right?" She looked my way and I waited for her to explain. "This all reminds me of 'An Inspector Calls'. Has anyone seen it?"

Anwar recalled some distant memory. "I think I read it at school. That's the one where the detective comes to a rich family and starts messing with their heads, am I right?"

"Not far off," Florence confirmed. "Izzy, is that what you're doing? Is this a sick joke at our expense?"

The room was quiet once more. I could see how eager everyone was for me to explain.

"Not quite. I admit that when I came in here this evening, I wasn't sure what had happened. I needed to see how you'd all react."

"See, she's been messing with us." Debbie had a unique talent for looking both happy and malicious at the same time. "I knew there was something not right with this one."

I soon cut her smugness short. "It didn't take me long to work it out though. And now I know, beyond any doubt, which one of you killed Birdy."

Winners and Losers

I'd been hoping that they'd get there without my help. I was too tired and sad to put on a show. I felt like coming straight out and saying who the murderer was, just like that, but it's not my style to do things by half.

Before going any further, I grabbed my phone and sent a one word text to my friend Ramesh back in Croydon. He already had instructions for what I needed him to do.

I stood up and walked to the long wall at the front of the building with floor-to-ceiling windows. I could see through the darkness that the water had dropped down to ankle height again. By the following morning, it would be gone completely and, if everything went to plan, so would I.

"Birdy told me something last night that I found very interesting." I turned back round to my audience. "She said that, her whole life, people had been inexplicably attracted to her. No matter how she acted, men would throw themselves at her and women wanted to be close to her.

"I wasn't sure I believed it at first; it sounded almost supernatural. But Birdy was a scientist, not a fantasist and, by the time I discovered her body, I'd come round to her way of thinking."

I walked back and placed both my balled-up fists on the end of the table. "We all have our abilities. I'm pretty good at spotting murderers these days and I make a mean bacon sandwich. There are people in the world who solve mathematical equations that most people can't begin to comprehend and conmen who spend their whole lives passing themselves off as other people without the slightest suspicion." I shot a smile in Mrs Gaskell's direction.

"So I'm willing to accept that Birdy had the unusual talents she claimed to. I came to Hastings to hide from the world but she yanked me from my shell. Everybody here was pulled towards her in one way or another.

"Anwar, you always felt inferior to her but I think ultimately what you wanted was her approval. When she didn't give it, she hurt you more than she had any right to. Florence, you trusted Birdy with all your secrets. She drove Roger up the wall and Malcolm always looked up to her so that the rest of you assumed he was in love. He said himself that he's not the romantic type so that only leaves one person."

Debbie flinched as I cracked open the last remaining can of beer. It had done its job and gently lubricated my suspects' tongues. "Debbie said that, despite their rivalry, she respected our departed friend and Birdy told me something very similar last night. Though Debbie was the only person here who could resist the pull of Birdy's exuberant personality, the two women acknowledged one another as equals and, in other circumstances might have been friends."

"What are you saying?" Debbie was alive to any hint of an allegation.

I walked over to her chair and knelt down so that we were eye to eye. "I'm just laying the groundwork; setting the scene. We're not there yet. First, tell me why you cried."

She tried to keep her voice flat. "I've already told you."

"No, when I first asked, you lied. Now you can tell me the truth. Why would you cry for a woman you didn't like?"

Her expression rock-hard, she returned my gaze but said nothing.

"That's okay. We'll come back to that a bit later." Before standing up, I whispered another comment in her ear. "If you hadn't cried, I'd never have known."

I walked back to my spot at the head of the table. "Roger was right about Birdy, she did have a boyfriend who was much younger than her. I didn't find out his name but she said he was gorgeous and phenomenally intelligent; further proof of her magnetism. She thought he'd be different from the relationships she'd experienced before but he turned out like all the others. He was needy, clingy, desperate for her attention and so she came down here to get away from him. An odd plan really, considering that one of the men in this room was just as obsessed with her."

Not one single mouth stayed closed right then.

Yay! I love it when they gasp.

I took my time, sipping my beer and inspecting their reactions one after another. Malcolm, Roger and Anwar were looking understandably nervous. "It was actually one of the first things she told me when we started talking yesterday morning. At the time, I thought it was an idle boast. The idea that people would constantly throw themselves at a heavyset woman in her seventies sounded unlikely. I didn't think anything of it until this afternoon when I was trying to make sense of Birdy's death."

I walked round the table to stand opposite Anwar. "Your wife's away on business a lot, isn't she, mate?"

Still fiddling nervously with his ring, he clearly wanted to protest but couldn't put the words together. "I don't see what… If you're suggesting I…"

"I'm not suggesting anything, I'm just stating a fact." I moved on to my next victim. "Malcolm, our loyal manager, it couldn't possibly be you. We all heard your emotional revelation. Which, now that I think about it, is a convenient thing to admit to in the middle of a murder enquiry."

Malcolm didn't seem upset by my hypothesis. "Convenient really isn't the word for it, thank you."

"Fine, I'll move on." I turned to face the last of the three men in the room. "Roger, who could blame you for looking away from home when your wife talks to you the way she does?"

Debbie didn't like that one bit. "Watch what you're saying!" Let's be honest, it was none of my business and I was being a nosy madam.

Occupational hazard, isn't it?

"Come off it, Debs. You called Roger a 'stupid little man' when you thought he got a question wrong in the quiz. You could give a praying mantis lessons in how to keep her man in line."

And despite all of that, Roger still had the need to put his hand on his wife's shoulder. Debbie looked like she was about to cry again and I felt a pang of guilt.

Snap out of it Izzy! Do you think Poirot ever felt bad for winding everyone up at the end of each book?

Roger backed up his actions with words. "You're talking nonsense. Debbie is a very good wife to me and if you're trying to say I was in love with Birdy then you've started to contradict yourself. It was only five minutes ago you said I hated her."

Ooh, he fell for it. Brilliant.

"No, I said she drove you up the wall. There's a big difference." I paused and glanced around the room. Only Florence appeared to be enjoying my performance. "What we all took for anger could just as easily have been passion. Love and hate so often overlap."

"Ridiculous! Re-dic-u-lus!" Roger blustered and complained but I could see from the expression on his wife's face that I was on the right track.

"Is it?" I'd been circling the table, proper TV detective style, and came to a stop opposite him. "For someone who claimed not to like her, you seem to know a lot about Birdy's love life."

Anwar clicked his fingers with excitement. "That's right! You were the only one who knew about the boyfriend, weren't you, Rog?"

"Doesn't prove anything. She must have mentioned it in passing."

"Nah, mate. We'd have remembered that."

"And what about you, Debbie?" I'm guessing from the barrage of questioning I'd unloaded on the Harrisons that most people in the room would have picked a prime suspect by this point. "You said that Birdy always took what wasn't hers. I wonder what you were referring to."

No doubt sensing where this was heading, Debbie had retreated within herself. Her fingers were closed together and I could tell that she wished her whole body could do the same and curl up in a little ball somewhere far away.

"That was the real reason you didn't like Birdy, wasn't it? You might have been friends if she hadn't stolen your husband away from you!"

Roger was up on his feet. "It's not true, is it, Debs?" But his wife couldn't respond with anything but tears.

I think this was the moment when Florence, Malcolm and Anwar realised that we weren't just playing a game. Birdy had been murdered and the killer was right there with us.

"You killed her!" It was Florence who threw the first stone. "You couldn't bear the thought of your man pawing another woman and so you took her out of the equation. Is that it?" She was really screaming and, with great effort, rose to standing in order to direct her fury all the more effectively. "You murdered one of the few people in the world who truly looked out for me."

Malcolm came to the old lady's assistance and walked her over to a chair by the wall. For a moment, the only sound was Debbie's tears.

I watched Roger to see how he might react but he didn't even come to his wife's defence.

"What were you thinking, Debs?" Anwar shook his head, almost sounding sad for the woman he believed to be a killer. "You knocked her out and cut her wrists then got rid of the evidence so that we'd think she'd done herself in. You killed Birdy."

"No, she didn't."

Our second gasp of the day!

Shhh! Why are you always so flippant?

I waited until everyone was quiet again before continuing. "At first, I thought that it was Debbie. The long-running animosity she shared with Birdy, and her hostility towards me today, was enough for that. But if she was the killer, there was one thing that didn't make sense. Debbie cried."

"She could have faked it," Malcolm suggested as I heard the first sounds of sirens in the distance.

"She didn't." My throat was sore. I'd been concentrating so hard on what was unfolding that I'd forgotten to breathe normally. "I watched her. I watched Debbie cry and I knew the pain she was in. Her heart had been broken and I considered every possibility. I thought perhaps that she was one who'd fallen for Birdy, just as so many others had before her, but that wasn't it. Debbie cried because she could see that our formidable neighbour would never have killed herself."

Breathe, one… two… three.

"Debbie cried because she knew that Birdy had been murdered and Roger was the killer."

End of Stay

I'd checked that there were no sharp objects around before I revealed the final twist. And I figured that Anwar could pretty much just sit on Roger until the police turned up. The quietly evil man didn't say a word as Malcolm tied his arms behind his chair with a bit of rope from the store cupboard.

"Why?" This was all Florence had been able to say since I'd unmasked the murderer.

"Birdy rejected you, didn't she, Roger?" Anwar was displaying the fierce temper that I'd been warned about. I hoped that the police would get there quickly before he turned violent. "You make me sick."

Roger didn't even show much emotion. He turned his head to one side and pretended not to hear. His wife couldn't bear to look at him anymore and was being comforted by Florence over near the exit.

"Was there even any relationship to hide? Or did you kill her because she never wanted you in the first place?" Anwar's words echoed about the room. I'd been wondering the very same thing.

It was just then that two police cars pulled up outside. The same tubby detective we'd seen that morning appeared, along with a uniformed officer who read Roger his rights. D.I. Stone looked sceptical that his original verdict of suicide would be disproven. There was no getting away from it though. When Debbie found her voice again, she'd be willing to back up the version of events that I'd pieced together.

I was confident that my theories would match the pathologist's report. There'd be signs of bruising on her body and the time of death would line up exactly with Roger's absence from his caravan the previous night.

The one thing I couldn't be sure of was why he'd done it. Perhaps he was so obsessed with Birdy that, when she refused his love yet again, he could see no other option than to cut her from his life. It was a mystery I couldn't solve alone and it didn't look like Roger was going to fill in the gaps. At least, not until he'd been found guilty in court.

When I watched him being taken away in handcuffs, he looked even fainter and less substantial than the first time we'd met. It was hard to imagine that such a person could have extinguished the firework that Birdy had been. He looked at me as he went, appearing neither upset nor pleased with himself. He was nobody; a nothing person I couldn't wait to forget.

Debbie left that night but I decided to stick around one more day. I honestly had great sympathy for her. She wasn't such a bad sort really, just protective of the man she loved. Maybe she'd have told the police her suspicions eventually anyway, if I hadn't stuck my oar in.

Saturday was Mexican Night at the caravan park just outside Hastings. The mariachi music and oversized sombreros were dispensed with that weekend though in place of frozen pizza, plenty of beer and lots of happy memories of Birdy Collins.

The profile she'd outlined of herself in our conversation didn't do her justice. Florence, Malcolm and Anwar put that right and filled my last night with countless wonderful stories of a friend who wasn't there to join in. And when I left the next morning, dragging my suitcase back along the muddy path where shallow puddles of rainwater still remained, the sun finally peeked out at me.

It didn't stick around for long.

The Izzy Palmer Mystery Series

"A CORPSE CALLED BOB" (BOOK ONE)

Izzy just found her horrible boss murdered in his office and all her dreams are about to come true! Miss Marple meets Bridget Jones in a fast and funny new detective series with a hilarious cast of characters and a wicked resolution you'll never see coming. Read now to discover why one Amazon reviewer called it, "Sheer murder mystery bliss."

Buy it now at amazon

"A CORPSE IN THE COUNTRY" (BOOK TWO)

One murdered millionaire, seven suspects and only forty-eight hours to work out whodunit. Izzy Palmer returns for another fast-paced and funny detective novel that delivers a contemporary spin on the golden-age country house mystery.

Buy it now at amazon

"A CORPSE ON THE BEACH" (BOOK THREE)

Spanish sunshine, pristine beaches and a bucketful of murder. A free holiday on the continent is too good an opportunity for Izzy to turn down. But the opulent Cova Negra Hotel, is not all that it seems. With bodies piling up and the police baffled, Izzy comes face to face with her deadliest adversary yet.

Available June 28th at amazon

Get your **Free** Izzy Palmer Novellas...

If you'd like to hear about forthcoming releases and download my free novellas, sign up to the Izzy Palmer readers' club via my website. I'll never spam you or inundate you with stuff you're not interested in, but I'd love to keep in contact. There will be one free novella for every novel I release, so sign up at...

www.benedictbrown.net

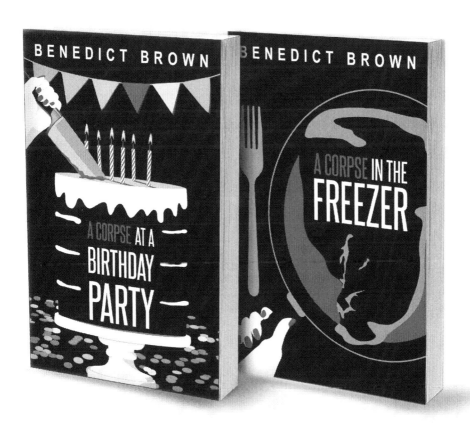

About This Book

First things first, if you haven't already read the first Izzy Palmer novel **"A Corpse Called Bob"** you could be enjoying it right now over at Amazon. It's filled with twists, laughs, a slightly odd detective talking to herself and I bet you don't work out who the killer is before the end – feel free to mail me to prove me wrong.

But back to the caravan… I started writing this novella after a conversation I had with my brother. To be honest, Daniel has always been the popular one in the family. It's a fact that drove me crazy as a kid and I could never understand why people flocked to him. Okay, I admit, my brother is funny, handsome and overflowing with charm but those positive qualities could be balanced out by a cruel sense of humour and moody personality.

It wasn't until this year that he revealed to me that making friends comes so easily to him that it doesn't matter how he acts. He explained that, at times, he has been almost intentionally unkind in order to test the limits of this ability. It was a strange confession to hear but it immediately got me thinking about a case for Izzy.

Regarding the setting, it's not based on a particular campsite but is no doubt informed by a trip to my friend Adam's caravan near Rye when I was about eight years old. I've never forgotten the curious collection of wonderfully British neighbours we had there. These two factors combined gave me the starting point for a mystery and I hope you've enjoyed **"A Corpse in a Caravan"**. Sign up to the Izzy Palmer **reader's club** to get your two free novellas and find out when the next novels are released.

Acknowledgements

I'm lucky to have the most incredible group of family and friends who have supported me in my writing for years. My wife and daughter have to get the first thank you, but I'll forever be indebted to my friend Lucy Middlemass who devoted so much time to helping me improve my books and has had a bigger impact on my ability as a writer than anyone else could. I will never stop imagining your response in the margins when I write a silly joke, Lucy. I hope it's funny, where you are.

A big thank you also goes to my murder mystery expert, Bridget Hogg, for reading and rereading Izzy's adventures, Karen for putting me on to the potential of the internet, my brilliant mother for thinking everything I write is great (sorry, Mum, I don't always believe you) and, okay, my brothers too for putting up with me. You are all brilliant humans and I love you very much.

About Me

I've been writing stories since I learnt how to hold a pen. I studied an MA in creative writing at **Aberystwyth University** and focussed for a long time on books for kids. The Izzy Palmer Mysteries are my first adult novels, in a genre which has always been special to me.

After university, I moved to **Spain** to be an English teacher, fell in love with a French woman and (12 years later) had an incredible baby. We live together in a pretty village, nestled among rolling hills and sunflower fields, near the medieval city of **Burgos**.

If you'd like to help me out, leaving positive reviews on my novel on Amazon can make a huge difference. High-starred reviews help independent authors like me stand out from a very crowded field. If you could spare the time, I would be phenomenally grateful.

If you'd prefer to tell me personally what you think of my writing, or have questions or feedback, I'd love to hear from you. Contact me via my website where you can sign up to my **reader's club** to hear about forthcoming releases...

www.benedictbrown.net

Printed in Great Britain
by Amazon

32616291R00036